WILD CURVES
WILD HEART MOUNTAIN: WILD RIDERS MC
BOOK FOUR

SADIE KING

WILD CURVES

WILD RIDERS MC

A fake relationship for a weekend between a biker who wants more and a shy girl who can't give him the one thing he craves...

Mom's coming to visit, and she expects to meet my new boyfriend. Spoiler alert: I don't have a boyfriend. I pretended I had one to get Mom off my back. I didn't expect her to show up on the mountain to meet him.

In steps Arlo, the bearded, tattooed biker I've been crushing on since I started working at the Wild Riders MC HQ. We'll pretend to be together to keep Mom happy. But as the weekend goes on, I'm falling for the easy-going ex-military biker.

But there's a reason why I don't date, and not even Arlo can change my mind.

Wild Curves is a fake relationship romance featuring an ex-military mountain man biker and the shy girl whose curves he can't get enough of.

Copyright © 2023 by Sadie King.

All rights reserved.

No part of this book may be reproduced in any form or by any electronic or mechanical means, including information storage and retrieval systems, without written permission from the author, except for the use of brief quotations in a book review.

Cover designed by Cormer Covers.

This is a work of fiction. Any resemblance to actual events, companies, locales or persons living or dead, are entirely coincidental.

Please respect the author's hard work and do the right thing.

www.authorsadieking.com

CONTENTS

1. Maggie — 1
2. Arlo — 13
3. Maggie — 20
4. Arlo — 28
5. Maggie — 35
6. Arlo — 43
7. Maggie — 51
8. Arlo — 57
9. Maggie — 65
10. Arlo — 75
11. Maggie — 80
12. Arlo — 88
    Epilogue — 96

Bonus Scene — 103
Wild Forever — 107
Books and Series by Sadie King — 113
About the Author — 115

1
MAGGIE

My hand shakes as I place the plate of chocolate-coated strawberries on the bar counter.

Arlo gives me an encouraging look that makes my insides flutter. I look away quickly, hoping he thinks my nerves are because of the dessert I'm presenting and not the fact that his luminous smile is turned on me.

"Let's give them a taste."

My attention snaps to Travis as he snags one of the strawberries and stuffs it in his mouth. He's the boss of the Wild Taste Bar and Restaurant and the person I have to impress if I want to get the pastry chef position once Patrick retires at the end of the year.

I hold my breath as he chews. His brows knit together and then raise in surprise.

"There's chili in these?"

I nod. "A little, to offset the sweetness."

"Mmmm..." Travis nods appreciatively. "These are good." He reaches for another one, and Kendra slaps his hand out of the way.

"Leave some for the rest of us."

She's the only one who can get away with playfully slapping the boss. He picks one up anyway and brings it to her lips.

Kendra opens her mouth to receive the strawberry and Travis pulls it away, just out of her reach. They both giggle and I look away, my ears turning pink at the intimacy of the moment.

Arlo catches my gaze and rolls his eyes heavenwards, making me smile. He works the bar and makes no secret of how sick he is of seeing Kendra and Travis all over each other since they got together.

I think it's sweet, the boss and the head waitress.

"What did you say these are called?" Arlo asks.

The blush spreads up my neck, and heat blooms in my cheeks.

"They're um... Strawberry Sin."

Arlo's eyes go wide, and a smile curls up his lips. "They taste like sin too."

As he says it he bites into the strawberry, breaking the chocolate seal with his teeth. My eyes dart to his lips. Lips so full they look indecent on a man. Lips so full they haunt my dreams as I imagine what they taste like, strawberry and chocolate with a hint of chili and cardamom. Sweetness and heat and something manly and exotic, which was my inspiration for the dessert. My knees go weak and my blush deepens.

"I need to get back to the kitchen and clean up."

I scurry away before the sight of Arlo enjoying the dessert that he was the inspiration for causes me to melt right onto the restaurant floor.

When I'm safely back in the kitchen, I lean so my forearms rest on the silver bench and let the coolness of the metal calm my heated skin.

All bartenders are terrible flirts, I tell myself. He likes my desserts and that's all.

Through the round window of the swinging kitchen door that leads to the restaurant, I watch as my three colleagues enjoy the rest of my strawberry sins.

I've been working at the Wild Taste Bar and Restaurant for three months now, and any normal person would be out there chatting and laughing with their colleagues. The last customer left a half hour ago, and while they've been out there enjoying their drinks, I asked if I could present Travis with a dessert I've been working on.

I should be out there socializing, but I prefer the cool steadiness of the kitchen. Especially after hours when everyone else has gone home.

My phone rings, and I stifle a groan when I see it's Mom calling.

I contemplate slipping it back in my pocket, but I've already missed two calls from her today. She'll get frantic if I don't pick up.

"Hi Mom."

"Maggie!" She screeches so loud that I pull the phone away from my ear. "I couldn't get hold of you."

"I'm working, Mom. Didn't you get my text?"

"You know I find it hard to read those things. Call me old-fashioned, but I prefer to talk."

Old-fashioned is definitely the word I'd use to describe my mother. And if this call is anything like the daily calls I get, I brace myself for what I'm in for.

"You work too hard, sweetheart. Make sure you leave time for yourself to have some fun."

I lick a bit of chocolate off my hand and try not to roll my eyes.

"Working is fun for me. I've invented a new dessert."

I try to sound upbeat, but as usual Mom pays zero interest to my professional life.

"You'll never meet anyone if you're working all the time, MeMe."

She uses my pet name from childhood and the stern but kindly tone that my mother has perfected.

It's incomprehensible to my mother that I would put my career ahead of meeting a suitable husband. This is usually where I tell her I don't want to meet anyone, and she gasps like she's having a heart attack. But I can't do it today.

We've had this same conversation for the last two years, since I went to culinary school and told her I wanted to be a pastry chef.

"And your uterus isn't getting any younger, sweetheart. Fertility starts to decline after thirty, you know."

The last is said in a whisper as if someone might hear her down the phone lines.

"Mom, that's not really true…"

"It is," she protests. "I read it in a magazine. These women putting their careers first…"

She launches into a tirade spoken in hushed but disapproving tones about 'these women' when what she really means is me.

"Mom…" I try to cut in to remind her that I'm

only twenty-three, but as always, I'm no match for my mother once she gets on a roll.

It's been a week of early double shifts, and the tiredness behind my eyes shifts to a full blown headache as I listen to my mom drone on. I press my fingers to my forehead and close my eyes, knowing from experience that it's best to let her run on until she's finished.

I love my mother, but it's the same lecture every week. Her first reaction when I told her I wanted to be a chef was how difficult the odd hours would be for raising a family.

I hadn't thought about that aspect of working life before. I just wanted to choose a career doing something I loved. Mom brings it up so often that I guess it's true.

As Mom drones on about the declining health of my ovaries, I watch Arlo through the window. He's chatting easily with Travis and Kendra, and a pang of longing jolts my insides. I shake it off. Mom's made it abundantly clear to me that if I want to be a pastry chef I'll never have a family. That's why I don't date. Even if the ridiculously handsome and charming bartender had an interest in small, tubby shy girls, there wouldn't be any point in dating him.

My head aches, and I want to get off this call with

Mom and find out what they really thought of my dessert and if Travis will put it on the menu. If only there was a way to get Mom off my back once and for all.

"I want a promise from you that you'll go out and make an effort to meet someone. Even Layla's got her own family now."

Mum's referring to my best frenemy. Layla's from the same town as me and went to the same culinary school. Layla opened her own cafe a few years ago and I'm always hearing about how she still made time to meet a man and start a family. I'm happy for Layla, I really am but running a cafe that's open in the daytime is different to being a pastry chef at a restaurant.

"She just had another little girl. You need to get yourself out there, the way Layla did."

My mom doesn't get it at all. There's a reason I took a job in the middle of a mountain. Here, I can focus on my career with no distractions. There's a bar in Wild that I've been to with Kendra once when she dragged me out. But hanging out with strangers is not my thing.

"Put on a short skirt, sweetheart. Don't be afraid of those thighs you inherited from me. Some men love chunky girls. Look at your dad!"

She cackles like we've shared a secret, and my belly churns as I try not to think about my dad checking out my mom's thighs. Never mind the reference to my short stumpy legs. I'm immune to Mom's thoughtless comments by now.

When I'm not experimenting with new dessert recipes or thinking about new dessert recipes, I'm watching cooking shows and, on my days off, visiting every restaurant and cafe in the area to see what they've got on the menu. I may be shy, but I'm focused and determined. And I will not promise my mom that I'll go to a bar to look for men.

"I'm not going out to a bar, Mom."

"Oh honey…"

There's disappointment in her voice and she takes a deep breath, but before she can start the next lecture, I jump in.

"I already met someone."

I clamp my mouth shut as soon as I say the words. There's silence on the other end of the line.

"Say that again?"

"I…uh… met someone." I swallow hard, hoping she doesn't hear the lie in my voice.

"You've met a boy?"

"Ya-ha." My palms start to sweat. I've never been a good liar, and Mom is suspicious as hell.

"Are you going steady? Is he your boyfriend?"

My eyes go to Arlo leaning casually against the bar, a smile peeping out from his thick beard. "Yup. I got me a boyfriend."

"Oh MeMe. That's fantastic," my mother gushes. I wish she'd been this happy when I told her I got into culinary school or when I won the creative dessert award.

"What's he look like? Is he hunky?"

"Umm…" My gazes slides over Arlo, and I take a step closer to the door so I can see all of him through the small round window. His head is tilted back in a laugh, the deep rumble of his chuckle reaching me through the kitchen door and doing weird things to my belly.

"Um, he's tall and he's got a beard."

"A beard!" Mom exclaims. "I guess that's what you young folk are all into. But I wouldn't have looked twice at your father if he had a beard. What's his name."

"Arl…" I start to say and snap my mouth shut just in time. My fantasy almost got away from me, but I'm not giving out Arlo's name to my mother. She'd probably look him up online.

"What's that honey?"

"Allan." I wince.

9

"Allan? Not a very romantic name, but you can't help that. Where did you meet him?"

"Umm…" My brain freezes and I regret even starting this lie, but I'm in too deep to back out now. The best lies have a grain of truth, so I decide to stick to some semblance of realness. Besides, she'll never know. "He works at the restaurant."

"He's not a chef, is he? Unsociable hours. It'll hard when you have a family."

"Mom…"

"Oh, I know, honey, I'm just so excited. Thinking about my grandbabies. Jim!"

She calls out to my dad, making me wince and wondering if I've just given her more fuel for the grandbaby pressure.

"Jim! MeMe's got a boyfriend!"

Dad mumbles something in the background. I don't know how my softspoken dad puts up with my mother. I've never met two such different people. Mom's loud and talks non-stop, while Dad's quiet and observant. I know which one I take after.

"We'll come visit this weekend and meet Allan."

Wait, what?

My attention snaps back to my mother. "You don't have to do that."

"Of course we do. My little girl's got her first

boyfriend. We have to meet this Allan and see if he's good enough for you."

Oh shit.

My palms sweat, and panic sets in.

"Um, we're both working this weekend. Double shifts."

"That's alright, honey. We'll look around the mountains. We've been meaning to visit and see the place. There's some good shopping in Hope, I hear. Hey, does Allan fish? Should Dad bring his rod?"

Oh my god, this got out of control real fast. My palm goes to my forehead as I try to backtrack.

"Um, I don't know. Please don't come. It's too soon…"

But as usual Mom barrels over me.

"We've been meaning to come and check out the Wild Taste Restaurant. Dad's worried that it's run by a MC."

"But…" I try to protest that the Wild Riders are ex-military and not into anything sketchy, but Mom cuts me off.

"Oh, I know what you're going to say, but your dad wants to check it out for himself. See what the club that employs you is all about."

I stride to the kitchen door and peer out through the round window. Arlo sees me and holds up the last strawberry.

"It's good," he mouths, and my stomach does a little flip.

"I gotta go," says Mom. "We'll see you Friday, MeMe. You and Allan."

I press my head against the door and close my eyes.

What have I done?

2
ARLO

I walk into the bar to prep for the lunch shift, and my breath hitches in my chest. I pause and lean against the bar, my gaze resting on the back of the woman who's haunted my dreams for the last three months.

How could she not? Maggie's short and curvy like a cute baby doll. She's quiet and shy, but I bet there are hidden depths behind her observant brown eyes, which dart away every time I catch her looking at me.

I haven't spoken to Maggie since she brought out the Strawberry Sins yesterday. It's no secret that the shy assistant cook aspires to move up in the kitchen. One of the perks of the job is trying out the new desserts she spends her spare time making. Travis is impressed, and I hope he gives her the promotion she deserves.

But it's not the Strawberry Sins I'm thinking of as I watch her at the table in the restaurant corner.

Maggie's positioned herself with her back to the bar looking out at the road and the view of the valley beyond. She must have been here early doing food prep and is taking her break before the lunch rush starts. Her chef's hat is sitting on the table, and strands of hair fall from her sloppy bun and trail down her neck. I'd love to sweep the tendrils up with my fingertips and feel the soft skin of her neck.

I'm not sure when I started having these thoughts about the shy assistant cook. I'm known for my ability to charm anyone, but every time I try to talk to her, she darts away. She's a mystery to me, one I'm dying to unravel.

But I'm a patient man. We're slowly getting to know each other, and I'll bide my time until she's ready.

I fix a hot chocolate with extra cream and marshmallows, her favorite, and take it over to the table.

She's staring intently at her phone and doesn't hear me coming. I don't mean to sneak up on her, but as I come closer, she huffs and lifts her phone up.

There's a picture of a bearded man with a face tattoo. She swipes left, and another man comes on screen, this one with a beard and a lopsided grin that promises far too much.

My blood floods with heat when I realize what she's up to.

"You're on a dating site?" The words slip out as emotion courses through me.

She spins around, making a surprised squeak, and her phone slips to the floor.

I've got no business getting in her business, but the thought of Maggie dating another guy has my blood boiling.

"Umm," she squeaks. "I was just having a look."

She leans down to get her phone at the same time as I do. I beat her to it and straighten up while holding the phone. With a few quick swipes, I've deleted the dating app.

"Hey, what are you doing?"

Her forehead puckers, and her eyes flare. No one likes their phone being fucked with, but if Maggie's going to date anyone, it's going to be me.

I've been patient because she's so shy, but I realize my mistake. She doesn't need to look for a man when she's got me right here.

"Too dangerous. You get all sorts of weirdos on those apps."

She glares at me as I hand the phone back. The

shy girl has a fiery side, and it looks like I've poked the mouse.

"I made you a hot chocolate."

The glare softens but only slightly. I've never seen Maggie cross before, and my dick twitches at the sight of her puckered eyebrows. I'll unpack that later.

Without being invited, I slide into the chair opposite hers.

Maggie doesn't strike me as the kind of girl to go out looking for a man. Kendra told me about the night they went out to a bar and how Maggie politely refused two drinks from strangers. Good girl. I made Kendra promise if they went out again to let me know, so I can make sure I'm there to watch over her. A sweet girl like Maggie has no business in a bar like the one in Wild.

Her cheeks are flushed a delicate pink that sets off the color of her plump lips.

She sips the hot chocolate, and a moustache of cream settles on her upper lip. Her tongue flicks out to swipe at the corners, and I have to stop myself from jumping across the table and licking the cream right out of her mouth.

"Why are you looking for a date?" It comes out as a growl that makes her eyes widen. It's a personal question, but I've got to know. If she's lonely, I'll take her out.

Maggie looks at me for a long while, her chestnut eyes seeming to access me.

She gives a long sigh and looks down at the table. "It's my mom."

I've noticed Maggie on the phone with her mom before, usually wincing with one hand pressed to her forehead.

"She's coming to visit this weekend."

"And you're looking to get yourself murdered before then so you don't have to see her?"

I say it as a joke, but I'm still pissed that she would risk her safety with someone she met online.

Maggie shakes her head slowly. "I wish it was that easy."

Her hands go to her face, and she groans. I wait for her to speak. In the three months since I've known Maggie, I've learned to talk less and listen more, which is hard for someone like me who likes to talk a lot.

"My mom's always hassling me for not having a boyfriend. So I kind of told her I had one."

She peers at me through the gaps in her fingers, waiting for my reaction.

A laugh bubbles up inside me as relief cools my bones.

"You're looking for an instant boyfriend?"

She cringes. "I know. I shouldn't have lied, but I didn't think they were going to come to check him out."

I laugh even more. She's distressed by the situation, but she's laughing too.

"And he has to have a beard and look like a murderer?"

"Murderer look is optional, but yeah. I might have said he has a beard."

I tug on mine, wondering if she thought about me when she was describing this imaginary boyfriend. Nah, I wouldn't be so lucky. Maggie is shy and determined. She's career focused and doesn't speak to anyone at the bar. In fact, she avoids me when she can. I'm dreaming if I think she thinks about me at all. But this is an opportunity I'm not going to miss.

"I've got a solution for you."

She sits back and eyes me skeptically. "Tell Mom I'm into girls to get her off my back?" She's funny when she's not being shy. I like the banter.

"If it's a fake girlfriend you want, then I can't help. But if you want a fake boyfriend…"

I sit back and press my fingers to my chest then open my hands while raising my eyebrows.

She stares at me, and her mouth drops open.

"You?"

"Don't look so horrified. I've got a beard, and I can charm anyone's mother."

I give her my best smile. I'm not a bar man for nothing. I love meeting people and can talk to anyone. That's how I got my road name: Prince. It's not because I'm royalty. It's because I'm Prince fucking Charming.

3
MAGGIE

"What did you just say?"

I can't have heard him right, because I think Arlo just said he'll pretend to be my boyfriend. Arlo's sitting with his arms out expansively and his eyebrows raised and a cheeky glint to his deep chocolate colored eyes. I've never noticed the amber flecks in them before, or the way they light up when he's laughing.

My heart skips a beat at the thought of Arlo pretending to be my boyfriend. Will he pretend to kiss me? The thought sends a bolt of heat through my body, jarring my thighs together. And I have to lower my eyes in case he reads the lusty thoughts in them.

It's ridiculous. He can't pretend to be my

boyfriend. I might like it too much. And I can't let my mother loose on Arlo. That wouldn't be fair.

"My mother would eat you alive."

He smirks, all manly confidence. "I can handle it."

He probably could too. Arlo is the friendliest person I know. He'll talk to anyone, which is why he makes a good barman. Which is why he's offering to help me out. It's not because he wants to help *me*. It's because he would help *anyone*.

"Are you working this weekend?" I ask.

I can't believe I'm even considering this harebrained scheme, but the other option is an unknown bearded man on the other end of an app that's no longer on my phone.

Better the devil you know and all that…

"I can swap my shifts."

"Don't do that," I say quickly.

If he's working, then that's better. My parents can come in to eat at the restaurant, because they're dying to see where I work. At least that's what Mom says, but I know she just wants to check out what the HQ of a motorcycle club looks like. She'll be disappointed if she's looking for a drug den and loose women. The Wild Riders MC aren't like that. They're a group of military veterans who love bikes and want to do good in the community.

The bar is decked out with motorbike memorabilia and there's always an impressive array of bikes parked out front, but other than that it's a classy place.

The brewery out back makes craft beer and the mechanic's isn't a front to launder money, at least not that I know of. I don't think the Prez would stand for that.

I've only been here for three months and I've barely talked to any of the men apart from those that I work with, but I can tell the Prez doesn't stand for any nonsense. He strides around with a set look and a sharp eye. He runs a legit business and doesn't suffer fools.

Arlo is eyeing me with a look of amusement that makes him look freaking adorable. I sigh inwardly. If I was a bolder type of girl, I'd know how to flirt with him. I'd bat my eyelashes and let him know I'm interested. But I'm not. I'm a small, tubby girl who prefers the company of food rather than people.

Besides, as Mother has pointed out so many times, with my career choice it will be impossible to have a family. There's a reason why most top chefs are men. Women drop out of the industry when they get to their child rearing years. I made my decision when I went to culinary school. If I have to choose between being a top pastry chef and having kids, I choose being a chef.

But when I look at Arlo, there's a pang of regret. I shake the feeling away. No point getting sentimental for a man who couldn't possibly be interested anyway.

My phone buzzing pulls me out of my reverie, and there's a message from Mom. She's really trying to get a handle on the text function.

Does Allan like blueberry muffins? We've got a good crop this year, and I'm baking

I glance up at Arlo, and he's eyeing me intently. A delicious shiver runs through my veins.

"Do you like blueberry muffins?"

His grin widens. "Sure do."

This is the chance to tell Mom it was all a lie, that I'm not seeing a bearded man called Allan, that I don't want a man and I don't want children. But I'm an only child, and that truth will break her heart.

Instead, I text back.

He loves them!

Arlo's grinning at me when I put the phone down, and if he wasn't so damn handsome this might be easier. I don't know how I'm going to get through a weekend pretending he's mine, when in reality he never will be.

"Fine." I place my hands on the table. "But there are ground rules."

Arlo leans forward, his eyes sparkling. "I've always been a rule breaker."

His eyes dart to my lips as he says it, sending a wave of heat rushing over me and making me lose my train of thought.

"Rule number one. No kissing."

His eyes dart to my lips, and he leans back. "I'm not promising anything."

Damn, his confidence sends my pulse racing. He's a natural flirt and must be used to girls falling all over him, not that I've seen him with anyone since I've been here.

"This is a pretend relationship for two days. There's no need to kiss."

"I disagree. You want to fool your parents, then you need to give them a show. Make them think you're passionately in love. If there's no physical affection, your mom will be calling you every day to ask if we've broken up yet."

He has a point, but he looks so damn smug when he says it that I'm sure he's trying to rile me up.

My eyes dart to his lips, and an image of his mouth on mine, his beard ticking my throat springs into my mind. I grab the side of the table to steady myself.

"No kissing, Arlo."

He doesn't agree, but he doesn't press the point. The thought of kissing Arlo has me so hot and bothered and flustered that I can't even think about what else should be in the ground rules.

There won't be a chance to kiss him if he's behind the bar working anyway.

"You meet them once. I'll bring them into work to see the place, and that's it. Answer their questions, be yourself. That's all you have to do."

He strokes his beard and thinks about it for a while.

"So, you want me to pretend to be your boyfriend, but I'm not spending time with your parents or kissing you?"

"That's correct."

He eyes me from under hooded eyelashes with a look that makes me squirm. He leans forward.

"Honey, if I was your boyfriend, I wouldn't be able to keep my hands off you. I'd want to meet your parents so I could ask them all about what you were like as a kid. Find out what your favorite doll was, what made you giggle, and what you were frightened of. Then I'd spend my life making sure you never had those fears and were surrounded by the things you love."

The words heat me up from the inside out. The smirk's gone from his face, and the look he's giving me is so intense that it's hard to look away.

My mouth drops open, and my tummy flutters. I can only stare at this man who's making me feel things I've never felt before. Things I don't want to feel.

My breathing is ragged, and I have to get out of here. I have to get back to the kitchen and the safety of the things I know. Arlo's making me want things that I can never have, things that I can never give a man.

I love the pretty words he's saying to me, but he's just flirting, I remind myself. Already playing a part.

"And if I was your girlfriend, I'd be up at 4 a.m. every morning for work. And when I work my way up to head pastry chef, it'd get worse. I'd work until midnight, I'd never be home for dinner, there'd be no date nights, no time for children, and you'd never see me."

His mouth drops open in surprise, and his eyebrows pull into a frown. I've wiped the smirk off his face, but it doesn't feel as satisfying as I thought it would.

I stand up abruptly.

"So it's just as well that this is a pretend scenario for one weekend only, because I'm not girlfriend material."

With that, I pick up my chef's hat and head back to the kitchen. I feel shitty, but it's best he knows straight up. There's no point in flirting with me. I've got no room for a man in my life.

4
ARLO

I watch Maggie's hips sway as she crosses the room and goes through to the kitchen without a backward glance.

I'm processing the unsaid message in her outburst. Maggie thinks she can't date because her job is too demanding. Fuck that. If she wants to work all the hours, I'll be waiting for her with a hot chocolate after every shift, no matter if it's the middle of the night.

Someone's given her this idea that she has to choose between her career and love. Maybe that's why she's immune to my flirting.

But if she thinks I'm not taking full advantage of this weekend, then she doesn't know me at all. The kitchen doors are still swinging shut when I go to find Travis in his office out back.

"I need a favor, boss."

We have a good relationship, and I'm a reliable worker and a member of the MC.

"What do you need?"

I love that there's no hesitation. That's what keeps me in the MC. We've got each other's backs. We're all military and know what that means. If anyone needs anything, someone will help out, no questions asked.

"I need the weekend off."

"Done," he says with no hesitation. "I'll get Davis to cover."

"Thanks, man."

"You going away?"

"Nope. I'll be around, but not working."

His eyebrows shoot up in an unsaid question. But when I'm not forthcoming, he doesn't push. I don't want everyone to know about Maggie and my charade, not until I can make it a reality.

"There's another thing... I need Maggie off her shifts too." His eyebrows shoot even further up his head. "But she can't know yet."

He peers at me, a suspicious smirk forming on his lips. "What are you up to, Prince?"

He uses my road name, maybe because he knows my scheme has something to do with a woman. The guys think I could charm the panties off a nun, which is why I'm Prince Charming. Not that I use my superpower for women. Not anymore.

There's only one woman I've been interested in since she walked into the restaurant three months ago, but my charm doesn't work on Maggie.

"I'm not going to divulge that."

His look turns stern. "You do anything to drive Maggie away, and I'll have your balls. She's the best worker I got, and I've got her pegged for promotion once Patrick retires in a few months."

The men here are as protective of the women as they are of each other.

I hold my hands up placatingly. "I don't plan on hurting her. Her parents are coming to town, and I want to make sure they have a good time."

It's kind of true. But I want to make sure Maggie has the best time. I want to give her the time of her fucking life and make her realize that I'm the man for her.

Travis shakes his head slowly. But he pulls up the schedule on his laptop.

"It'll be tight, but we can manage." Travis narrows his eyes at me. "I don't know what you're up to, Arlo, but if I have to choose, you'll be fired and not Maggie."

Travis is a tough talker but he's also a softy for

love, having recently found it himself. I give him my best grin.

"Thanks, boss. Appreciate it."

"You got a date or something?"

Snips smirks at me as I slide into the barber's chair two days later. It may have been six months since I last had a haircut, but I'm not going to divulge my reasons for coming in here today.

"Can't a man get a haircut for no reason other than wanting to look respectable?"

"Not when it's as infrequent as you," he quips.

I chuckle at the banter, but he's right. If it wasn't for the pretend relationship with Maggie, I wouldn't be in here for another few months.

I enjoy the banter with Snips while he cuts my hair and trims my beard. I want to make a good impression this weekend. Not because I give a shit what her parents think of me, but I do care that they give her a break.

I've noticed how often her mom calls and the long conversations Maggie has with her. Maggie's a quiet girl, and I've drawn her out of her shell over the last few months. Once she gets to know you, she'll talk about anything, but after those calls with her mom she retreats back into herself, as timid as a mouse.

I'm curious to meet her mom, and if I can deflect any heat away from Maggie I will. Which is why I'm getting myself tidied up. I mean to make the most of my fake dating weekend.

Snips is finishing off my beard when his phone buzzes. It's on the countertop, and he checks the number and frowns. His mouth sets in a grim line as he pointedly ignores the buzzing phone.

It finally stops, and his shoulders relax. He's reaching for the beard oil when it rings again. His hands rub together too vigorously, and when he rubs the oil into my beard, he's so rough that it pulls on my hair.

"You gonna get that?" I ask.

"Nope."

He doesn't offer any explanation and I usually wouldn't push, but when it rings a third time, a volley of curses comes out of his mouth.

"The tax man chasing you or something?"

Snips frowns. "Worse than that."

At the same time, the baby monitor that's sitting on the counter springs to life. Cries flood the room, and Snip's face goes soft.

"That's you done," he says. "Knew I could fit a customer in during her afternoon nap."

"You've got the kid here?"

Snips recently found out he was a dad. It was a shock to him when social services called informing him he was the closest relation since the mother passed.

Snips was a little wild every time we came back from tour, and it caught up with him eventually. He got a paternity test done, and it's official. Three months ago, he became a dad to a cute one-year-old baby girl.

"I got the crib set up out back."

He goes through a door and comes back a few moments later cradling his little girl. In the arms of her daddy, the cries peter out. She grabs at his beard and giggles.

I have a sudden image in my mind of Maggie holding our baby in her arms as she looks down on her. It's a nice fantasy and my chest swells with the knowledge that that's what I want.

"That phone call got something to do with the baby?"

Softened by his daughter, Snips gives a long sigh. "Yeah, turns out Karen had a sister. She's threatening to get custody."

With his free hand, he expertly grabs a container of sandwiches and hands them to the baby.

Three months ago, the shock of being an instant

dad had him reeling. Now he'd do anything for his little girl.

"They can't take her away from you, can they?"

He sighs. "Trying to say because I wasn't there for the first year of her life that she's better with the sister."

There's pain in his voice, and I feel for the man.

"Where was this sister when Bailey's mother died?"

"Good point. Social services have been cagey. They won't give out details, but there's got to be some reason why she didn't step in at first. I didn't even know Bailey existed. I would have been none the wiser."

He pulls her close as if the thought makes him hurt.

"If you need anything, just ask, okay?"

"Thanks, man. I already got Trish and Danni babysitting a few days a week. I'm working reduced hours here, so we're managing."

There're dark circles under his eyes, and I wonder how well he really is managing. I make a note to bring it up with Prez and see if there's anything the club can do. I leave him with his daughter while I head across the mountain to Hope in search of a new outfit to wear this weekend.

5
MAGGIE

Friday comes around too soon. It's a busy lunch shift with a tour group in, and my palms are sweaty as I drizzle the chocolate sauce over the fudge cake under Patrick's watchful gaze.

"Lift the dish high to get the drizzle thin at the edges of the plate." Patrick indicates what he means and I lift the dish up, pleased to see him smile as the sauce makes a zig zag pattern around the edges of the plate.

He's the best pastry chef I've worked for, and even though I'm meant to help out everywhere in the kitchen, Chef lets me help Patrick as much as I can.

We're almost at the end of the service when I hear her. You can't not hear my mother. Her booming voice penetrates the kitchen doors and makes my hands tremble so much that I drop the dish of sauce and it clatters to the floor.

"Never mind," says Patrick as I duck to pick up the pieces. "That's the last one for this service anyway."

I dump the broken pieces in the trash and peek through the round window to the restaurant. Sure enough, there's Mom, her brown hair perfectly coiffed with so much hairspray even a strong mountain wind couldn't move it. Dad stands quietly behind her, his hands in his pockets as he rocks back on his feet, admiring the vintage bike on display in the corner.

Mom's chatting with someone at the bar, and my pulse spikes thinking it must be Arlo. I tilt my head to see more through the window and frown when I see Davis behind the bar. Davis is one of the prospects and he looks terrified as mom talks at him, probably telling him about all about their journey here and complaining about the traffic.

Arlo was supposed to be working so I could briefly introduce him to my parents and then keep them out of his way for the rest of the weekend.

Maybe he's coming in later for the evening shift. Whatever it is, I need to get out there so I can control the situation.

"My parents are here." I take my apron off and hang it up before smoothing down my hair. Chef said it was okay to leave early once my parents turned up so they could have lunch at the restaurant before the service finishes.

Dad sees me first.

"Hello love." He pulls me into a hug and kisses my cheek. We share a warm look before Mom turns around.

"What happened to your hair?"

Her look of horror has me ducking my head and smoothing down my hair. It's flat where my chef's hat was, but the way Mom's looking at it, I may as well have dyed it purple.

"It's just where the hat…"

"I've got spray in my bag." She takes me by the elbow and leads me to the side of the bar near the corridor that leads to the back entrance. There's no point resisting.

"We need to get some volume into that, MeMe. You can't go around all day with flat hair. What will Allan think?"

Ah yes, Allan. I thought Arlo would be working the bar today, and I'd be able to introduce them before we have lunch and then keep them out of the restaurant for the next two days. But he's frustratingly not here.

"Um, I don't think he's working today."

Mom's face falls. "You mean he's not joining us for lunch?"

She sprays my hair and runs her fingers through it, tugging at the strands. My hair has always been a disappointment to my mother. It's thin and mousy brown like Dad's, not the thick almost black tresses that are Mom's crowning glory.

"No," I say with finality, ducking my head away from her. "He is not."

"He's not what?" A booming voice comes from behind me, and I turn around to find Arlo striding toward us.

He's dressed in smart black jeans and a tight white t-shirt that hugs his muscles under his Wild Riders MC leather jacket. His hair is slicked back and his beard neatly trimmed so it frames his cheeky grin to perfection.

My mouth drops open, because he's not dressed for work and he's not behind the bar.

While I'm wondering what the hell he's doing striding in looking like my hot date, he marches up to me, slides his arm around my waist, and pulls me to him.

I gasp in surprise, but before I can say anything his mouth is on mine. His lips press against mine while my wide eyes stare into his laughing ones. His tongue flicks between my teeth, and his grip on my waist tightens.

Heat surges through my body. My heart hammers against my rib cage, and a delicious feeling of longing envelops me. My eyes flutter closed and I part my lips, letting his tongue tangle with mine. Our hips bump together, and the heat surging through me feels so damn good. My hand moves to his neck, and my fingers tangle in the hair at the nape of his neck.

Someone coughs, and I remember where we are and what we're doing.

This is a show kiss in front of my parents, nothing to get carried away about. I pull away quickly, but Arlo won't let me out of his grasp. He keeps his hand firmly around my waist.

My mother is speechless, and my dad looks like he wants to kill Arlo. Which is something for my mild mannered dad.

"This is, ah, Allan," I say, pressing my fingers to my lips. They're swollen and tingling and aching to kiss him again.

Arlo gives me a look at the name, and I dig him in the ribs.

"Hi, I'm Allan," he says with a grin, holding his hand out to Mom.

"Allan." Mom finally finds her voice. "So nice to

meet you. I'm Debbie and this is Jim."

Dad reluctantly shakes Arlo's hand, his gaze darting to where Arlo's clasping my waist, his hand inches away from my butt.

"It's nice to finally meet you," Arlo says, his charming smile already working on my mom. "Maggie's told me so much about you."

"She has?" Mom gives a flattered smile, unaware she's falling under Arlo's charm.

Dad's observing him quietly. He's not going to be won over by a big smile and easy charm. Arlo indicates the vintage bike that Dad was looking at.

"It's an original Harley, one of the first off the production line."

Dad raises an eyebrow. He's impressed, and I relax a little. "She still go?"

"We ride her once a year for the veterans charity run on July 4th."

They fall into step together talking bikes as Arlo leads everyone across the road to the VIP area where there's a reserved table. It overlooks the valley below, the view stretching all the way to the next mountain range.

Mom grips my arm and drops her voice to a whisper.

"Oh MeMe, he's divine."

My eyes are on Arlo's butt in the tight jeans walking in front of me.

"Yeah, he's…"

"And those muscles…" Mom inhales sharply. "The tattoos. I bet he's rough in bed."

"Mom!" My cheeks instantly heat, and Mom cackles.

Arlo and Dad turn to stare at us.

"We're just having some girl talk," Mom says, wiggling her eyebrows at Arlo in what I assume she thinks is a sexy way but instead looks like caterpillars are dancing on her forehead.

I'm so horrified I wish the ground would swallow me up. But Arlo just laughs and winks at Mom.

"Did she tell you where I've got my secret tattoo?"

Mom's mouth drops open and she turns to me, deliciously scandalized.

"She did not."

I've got no idea what Arlo's talking about, but he's grinning like the Cheshire Cat. Luckily at that moment, we arrive at our table. I note Arlo's reserved the best spot in the house.

Arlo holds the chair out for Mom, winning her over even more.

"You in town for long?" he asks once we're seated.

"Just for the weekend."

"Perfect. What do you want us to show you while you're here?"

I nudge Arlo under the table, because he's not showing them anything. "What a shame you have to work, honey."

He fixes his gaze on me. "I don't. I got the weekend off."

"That's so good of you," Mom gushes, while I stare daggers at him. He keeps looking straight ahead, talking to Mom about the places of interest they might want to visit.

"I didn't know you had the weekend off," I say tightly.

"Of course. I wouldn't miss spending the weekend with your parents."

"That's so sweet of you," Mom gushes, while I kick him under the table.

He was supposed to have a quick meeting with them. Let them know he existed before spending the weekend conveniently working. But for some reason Arlo wants to taunt me. The problem is, I'm kind of enjoying having him around.

6
ARLO

*I*t's late in the afternoon by the time we finish our leisurely lunch. Leisurely because I insisted on drawing it out by getting Maggie's father the tasting menu from the brewery. We've talked over the finer points of ale versus bitters and I've shown him around the bar, focusing on the vintage bikes we've got on display. Turns out her dad's an enthusiast and an easy man to talk to. He's got the same softly spoken mannerisms as his daughter and the same quick intelligence.

We've come back across the road so I can show Jim the bikes on display, and Debbie's voice carries from where the girls are sitting at the bar.

"I'm not saying there's anything wrong with wearing a chef's hat, but it will give you split ends.

It's not good for the hair to be squashed down all the time."

While I love chatting bikes with Jim, it's time to rescue my girl. No wonder she doesn't talk much with her mother always at her.

"Where are you staying?" I ask, not caring that I cut into Debbie's tirade.

Debbie looks at me and back at her daughter. "We're staying with you, aren't we MeMe? I didn't book a hotel." She turns in her seat and calls across the room. "Jim, did you book a hotel?"

Jim shakes his head and goes back to studying the pictures hanging on the wall.

"I thought you wouldn't mind having us at your place. We haven't seen you in so long. But if you don't want us there, I'll find a hotel."

She sniffs, and Maggie puts her hand over her mom's quickly. "It's okay, Mom. You can stay at my place."

I'm beginning to see why Maggie comes across as shy, living under the shadow of her mother all the time. She's too nice for her own good. But it gives me an idea.

"That's settled then. You can follow us on my bike."

Maggie gives me a look like she wants to throttle

me, but Debbie's too busy fluffing her hair to notice. "Come on, babe. The bike's out back."

Maggie stares at me for a long time and I give her a wicked smile, not sure if it's the term of endearment or the bike that's got her rattled. Either way, I like seeing the fire in her eyes. It makes my dick twitch thinking about her simmering energy in the bedroom.

I hold my hand out, and Maggie ignores it as she slides off the bar stool. Her parents follow us out the back to the courtyard.

I snag Maggie's hand and clasp it firmly in mine. She digs her nails into my palm, but I don't let go. She wanted me to play her boyfriend, so I'm doing just that.

Her parents get into their car, and I lead Maggie over to my bike. As soon as we're out of earshot, she drops my hand.

"What are you doing?" she hisses, her eyes sparking fire at me.

"Giving them a show and getting them off your back. It's what you wanted, isn't it, babe?"

"Don't call me that." She crosses her arms in front of her chest and marches in front of me, her short legs working overtime in her huff.

She stops in front of a large road bike and grabs the helmet.

"I've never been on a bike before."

A thrill goes through me. I love that I'll give her her first ride. "You'll be fine. But that's not my bike."

"Damn." She puts the helmet down in a huff and follows me to my Harley Roadster.

I pull my spare helmet out and give it to Maggie. She slips it on her head but hesitates before getting on the bike.

"Come on." I pat the seat. "Hold onto me, and you'll be fine." I lean toward her until my breath is tickling her ear. "I'll take it slow for your first time."

She dips her head, and a pink tinge blooms on her neck. I love making my girl blush.

It's her parents pulling up in their car that makes her get on the bike. Her hands hold the side of the seat, and I take them in mine and bring them around the front so she's clasping me around the middle. The action makes her body slide forward and press into me, just where I want it.

"Awww." Her mom rolls down the window and holds her phone up. "I've got to get a picture of you two."

I give her my best grin as she takes a couple of pictures, keeping Maggie's hands clasped to my body so she can't pull away.

"I'll get you for this, Arlo," she mutters, which makes me chuckle. "No more dessert for you."

I laugh harder. "Oh babydoll, you are dessert."

Before she can make a sassy comment, I rev the engine and pull out of the compound. Maggie clings on to me, and I take it slow until I feel her relax. It's a beautiful afternoon, and the view is stunning as we wind down the mountain road.

"So, where do you live?" I ask into the comms system. Maggie startles, and I chuckle.

"There are comms in here?"

"Yup. How else am I going to hear your beautiful voice?"

I can practically hear her eye roll. "You can stop pretending now, Arlo. My parents aren't around to hear."

"I'm not pretending, baby."

She sighs like she doesn't believe me. She thinks I'm messing around, but that couldn't be further from the truth. I've been waiting for an opportunity to make this shy girl mine, and I'm not wasting it.

"23 Hildon Drive. The block of apartments."

She chooses to ignore my comment, which is fine for now. She'll come around later when I have her in my cabin.

I know the address. It's a back road of Wild, and it doesn't take long to get there.

We pull up out front of the shabby looking apartment block. The gate is hanging off its hinges, and there's litter strewn across the courtyard.

"You live here?" It's so different than my cozy cabin nestled in the woods.

"Yeah." She sticks her chin out defiantly. "It's cheap."

It looks cheap. And too damn run down for my woman. I'll move her out of here as soon as I can. As soon as she agrees to be mine.

Her parents pull up, and we head to her ground floor apartment. Despite the run down exterior, Maggie's made the inside of her apartment homey. The walls are a light lavender color, and the place smells of berries and chocolate. The small kitchen is crammed with her cooking gear, and recipe books take up every spare surface.

There's a bed in one corner and a couch in the other.

"You two can have the bed, and I'll sleep on the couch."

Her mom looks around in dismay and Maggie looks down, clearly preparing herself for a lecture. But for once it doesn't come. Maybe her mother's finally at a loss for words.

I had no idea Maggie was living in a place like this. She twists her hands as she looks around, clearly embarrassed.

"It's all I need," she says simply. "It's perfect for a single woman." Her mouth snaps shut as she realizes her mistake.

But Debbie's too sharp. "Will you be moving in together soon?"

Jim holds his hands up. "There's no rush, sweetheart. You don't have to move in until you're married."

He looks at me pointedly, and behind the calm and quiet exterior I glimpse the same fire that Maggie hides.

"We're not getting married," Maggie says quickly, gaining a sharp look from her mother.

"Not yet," I say, grabbing Maggie's hand in mine. "But I want you to know, my intentions toward your daughter are serious."

Debbie beams, and Maggie gives me a dirty look.

"Let's give these two some space, babe." I pull her toward the door before her mom can ask any more awkward questions.

"But where are we going?"

"You're staying with me for the weekend." Excitement flashes across her face before she rearranges it into a disapproving look. She's trying to stay cross with me, but her defenses are weakening.

Debbie claps her hands together. "We can go to a hotel; I don't want to put you out."

"It's not putting me out. We stay most nights at my place anyway."

Jim scowls at me, but Debbie beams. Maggie looks like she wants to kill me, but she puts on a smile and follows me outside.

"We'll see you two tomorrow." I wave as we shut the door.

As soon as the door's shut, Maggie throws my hand down and strides to the bike. I watch the sway of her angry hips. She's coming to my cabin. Now I just need to figure out how to get her cute ass into my bed.

7
MAGGIE

It's a weird feeling, to be cross with someone and at the same time turned on by them. This is the feeling I have as my thighs wrap around Arlo's bike. My hands are around his waist and my body presses into him, the vibrations of the bike adding to the heat coming off his body. The trembling in my thighs has only half to do with the bike and more to do with the man whose body I'm pressed up against.

It's the audacity of it that I can't get over. He knows I didn't have a choice but to come back here once he suggested it. To refuse would have given away the fact that this is all a sham. He's taking advantage of the fake relationship scenario to purposefully make me uncomfortable.

I've had people tease me all my life for being too

short, for being too tubby. And now there's Arlo with his overly kind words, pretending that he's not pretending. It's just another way to tease me.

If I didn't find him so damn attractive, it would be easier. But I'm about ready to jump his bones. Especially with this machine humming under me and making my virgin pussy flutter.

If it wasn't working so damn well with my mother, I'd slide right off this bike right here and now. But Mom's falling for it hook, line, and sinker, and I have Arlo to thank for that.

If it wasn't for him, she'd be harassing me about every man we passed on the street. If I can just get through this weekend, if I can weather his teasing, and if I can make it through with my heart and my virginity intact, it will all be worth it.

The bike slows, and we pull onto a tree-lined gravel path. There're flashes of brown through the undergrowth, and his cabin comes into view. It's made of slatted logs, a classic log cabin nestled amongst the trees.

On the front porch are two red wooden chairs, and a string of fairy lights hang off the eaves. It's cozy and welcoming and looks like a real home after the concrete slab that is my apartment block.

Arlo pulls the bike to a stop out front, and I slide off the back before he can help me. My foot catches on something, and I stumble. Arlo reaches out a hand to steady me, but I bat him away.

"I'm fine."

"I know you're cross with me, Maggie. But there was no way I was going to leave you in that small apartment with your mother. I might as well leave you in a lion's den."

He's right. I know he's right. And that makes it all the more infuriating. I want to be cross with him. But the truth is, his thoughtfulness is working its way into my heart.

Stupid heart.

I slam my heart closed before I can make this any more complicated than it already is.

"It's fine," I say, and this time meaning it. "Thank you."

Arlo shows me into the cabin, and my breath catches in my throat. The kitchen is huge. A large marble work bench, perfect for rolling pastry takes up almost half the kitchen area. Metal utensils hang from the rafters, and there's plenty of spare bench space for all of my supplies.

Hold up, I remind myself. *It's not like you're really moving in here.*

Large windows look out over the green forest and the darkening sky. Stairs lead up to a second level.

"You live here alone?"

It's a big space for one person, but I've never seen Arlo with anybody. I hate the way I hold my breath waiting for his answer.

"For now."

He eyes me as he says it, giving me his cheeky grin. My heart flutters, but he's only teasing me, and it has to stop. I may have trouble standing up to my mother, but I'm not going to let Arlo mess with me.

"I don't know what game you're playing, Arlo, but it's not nice of you to tease me like that."

His face falls. "I'm not teasing you, Maggie. I'm not playing."

He looks sincere. But how can he be? I'm too short, too tubby, and my hair's too flat, as my mom never tires of pointing out. There's no way a man like Arlo would be into someone like me. And even if he was, I'm not interested. I've got my career to think of.

"Just show me to the spare bedroom." I sigh heavily. I've had enough of these games. "Thank you for pretending, but you don't need to pretend anymore."

He looks at me long and hard and lets out a big breath.

"She's really done a number on you, huh?"

"Who has?"

He pushes off of the kitchen counter that he's

leaning against and walks towards me. The closer he gets, the more I have to tilt my head back so I can see him. He only stops when our toes are almost touching.

A meaty hand reaches down, and he takes a strand of my hair and tucks it behind my ear. The gesture is so simple and so sweet it makes my heart flutter in my chest.

"Your hair looks cute under the chef's hat," he says. "You're a beautiful woman, Maggie, and a talented chef. I wish your mom could see that."

I'm frozen in place, looking up at him. I want to believe him. I do. My heart's racing as his thumb skims my cheek.

"If you're fucking with me, Arlo, this is going too far."

His thumb brushes against my lip, and I gasp at the sensation.

"I'm not fucking with you, Maggie. I've wanted you ever since you started working at the restaurant. I'm not pretending."

His hand slides around the back of my head, and he tilts my face up to him. My lips part as my heart hammers against my rib cage.

"I want you here in my cabin always, babydoll."

His lips press against mine and a tingle spreads through my body all the way down to my toes. He tastes like coffee and cake and temptation. And I can't get enough.

His body moves towards me, until I feel my breasts press against his muscular chest. The kiss deepens and his hand slides down my back, pulling me toward him until I bump against something hard.

I gasp in surprise when I realize what it is. But not before my body has a response that I can't control. Wet heat surges between my legs. My pussy flutters and I grind myself against him, wanting him, needing him.

Then I remember where I am, and all the reasons why I can't be with a man. Why I shouldn't lead him on. My eyes flick open, and I slip out of his grasp.

"I can't, Arlo."

Disappointment clouds his face as I back away. My insides churn. He felt so freaking good, but I can't go any further. I've spent too long on my career; I won't give it up for a man. And it wouldn't be fair to him.

"Maggie…"

Arlo takes a step toward me and I hold my hand up, cutting him off.

"I'm sorry, Arlo. You're my fake date, nothing more."

Hurt flashes across his face, but I turn and flee up the stairs before I do something I regret.

8
ARLO

It's hard to sleep when there's a pint sized goddess in your spare room. Somehow, I make it through the night without ripping Maggie's door down and ravishing her. I had a taste of her lips last night, and I'm hungry for more. But she needs time.

I don't believe I'm nothing to her. The way she kissed me yesterday with hunger and passion told a different story. I need to convince her we're meant to be together.

Maggie doesn't realize how damn gorgeous she is. She's a queen, and today I'm going to treat her like one.

I'm up early to make breakfast, hoping the smell of bacon will lure her out of the spare room. When she doesn't come out of her room, I make up a tray and take it to her.

"Maggie?"

There's no response when I knock on the door, so I push it open a crack and call again.

The shower's running in the adjoining bathroom, so I put the tray down on the bedside table. She's only slept in here one night, but her scent lingers, icing sugar and sweetness and something feminine and floral.

I'm about to leave when the shower turns off, and a moment later she comes through the bathroom door.

Maggie's wrapped in a bath towel, her wet hair plastered to her cheeks. Water droplets glisten on her chest, and the mounds of her breasts swell above the line of the towel.

My mouth goes dry as I cast my eyes over her. She might be pint sized, but she's perfection, her curves bursting out of the towel.

My dick hardens, and I should go. I should turn around and leave and give her privacy. But I'm rooted to the spot. She looks too good to back away from.

"I brought you breakfast."

She pulls the towel tighter around her chest,

causing it to ride up her thighs. If she's surprised to see me in her room, she doesn't show it.

I walk to the door, but I can't leave. I came in here to tell her how I feel, and wrapped in a towel or not, I intend to do just that.

"Maggie, I'm not teasing you. I want you to believe that. I'm not pretending. I want you to be my woman, Maggie. I don't want to pretend. I want you."

Her eyes go wide, and pain flashes in them.

"I can't get involved Arlo," she says with finality.

"Why? What's the problem?"

"I can't get involved with anyone. I want this promotion when it comes up. I've worked too hard."

Relief floods me. If that all she's worried about, then I can solve that. She doesn't have to give up her career, but I can tell there are no words that will convince her right now. But maybe my tongue can.

I stride towards her until I'm taking up her space, the flimsy towel all that separates us. Her eyes widen, and her lips part.

My hand runs over her bare shoulder.

"I don't want you to give up your career. You make the best desserts I've ever tasted."

She smiles shyly at the compliment.

"But let me taste you. Let me make you feel good, like you deserve."

My arm wraps around her body, and I pull her toward me.

"Let me take care of you, Maggie, right here, right now. Give me the weekend. Let me show you what being with me can be like."

She's breathing hard as she pushes away from me, torn between what she wants and what she thinks she should do.

My hand grasps the top of the towel, and I yank it off her. Maggie gasps, and her arms cover her body. Her cheeks flush, but I don't give her time to be embarrassed.

My hand slides between her legs, and she's dripping wet.

"You're beautiful, Maggie."

Her head tilts back, and I kiss the skin of her throat as my fingers slide between her folds.

"Tell me you want me to stop."

She whimpers in my arms and presses her hips so my palm rubs against her clit.

"Don't stop, Arlo."

I push her gently back on the bed and let my mouth travel down her body. My hand follows, running over every curve of her torso, feeling the texture of her skin against my rough hands. Her beautiful breasts, the softness of her stomach, the curve of her hips, and the soft downy triangle of hair between her legs. I feel the heat coming from her core as I press my palm between her legs.

"Let me take care of you, Maggie. I need to hear you say it."

I look up at her, and she's panting hard.

"Yes," she whimpers. "For the weekend."

I want forever with this woman, but if she's only prepared to give me a weekend, then I'll take it.

I slide my palm to the hotspot between her legs where she's wet and sticky from the shower and her own juices blending together.

I drop to my knees, licking her nipples and belly until I'm between her thighs. As I run my tongue over her glistening folds, she lies back on the bed propped up on her elbows.

"Relax, Maggie. I'm gonna take care of you."

I keep one hand strumming her nipple as I duck my head between her thighs. Her pussy tastes divine and I devour it with slow movements, sucking and licking and kissing her most sensitive parts. My other hand pushes her thighs open until her flower blooms for me. She's beautiful, the soft pink like a ripe strawberry ready for picking. It's the sweetest sight I've ever seen.

My finger runs through her folds, and I slide a digit into her pink opening.

She's so tight it makes my dick ache. Thinking

about being inside her is pure torture. But it's too soon. I promised I'd take care of her this weekend, and that's what I intend to do.

My finger glides in and out of her opening as my tongue licks her sweet folds.

She's the sweetest dessert, and I devour every single drop of her.

Lifting up her leg, I sling it over my shoulder and she opens up, moaning in pleasure. The shy girl is gone as she writhes on the bed, letting me devour her sweet, sweet nectar.

"Arlo…" she pants, and I love the way she says my name. "Something's happening."

Something in her tone gives me pause, and I lift my head.

"Have you ever done this before, babydoll?"

She shakes her head. "I'm a virgin."

My dick strains against my pants. Sweet Jesus, she's everything a man could want served up on a platter before me. Mine for the taking, mine to devour, mine to look after.

I want so bad to pop that sweet cheery, but I'm a patient man. I'll make her ache for me first.

"Just relax. The pressure's gonna build, and you're gonna come, and it's gonna feel so fucking good. Just remember who it is making you feel so good."

I pinch her nipple as I say it, and she mewls. I dip my head between her thighs, sucking and lapping, my fingers fucking her tight cunt until I feel her pussy flutter and convulse, squeezing my fingers tight.

Her juice explodes on my tongue, and I glance up. Her beautiful face is scrunched up, her jaw shut tight, too afraid to make a noise. I'll change that. By the end of the weekend, I'll have her screaming my name so loud it'll rattle the windows.

Her body's trembling, but I'm not done yet. I want her thighs coated in juice and her knees wobbling when she leaves my cabin.

I press my face against her pussy again, and I don't let up until her body shakes and another orgasm claims her.

Only then do I pull away.

"I've never done that before," she whispers, her voice filled with wonder.

God, she's so perfect. I climb onto the bed next to her and pull her into my arms. My cock's aching for release, but it will have to wait. I want my girl to feel good this weekend. I said I'll take care of her, and that's what I'll do.

I kiss the top of her head and point to the plate of food still warm on the bedside table.

"Eat. You'll need your strength today."

Her brow furrows. "Why?"

She slides the tray onto the bed and attacks the eggs. Watching her eat makes me smile. My girl's got an appetite.

"I've booked your parents on the brewery tour at ten. And then I thought we'd check out one of the mountain trails."

She stares at me, a piece of bacon in one hand. "You're coming today as well?"

I give her my best grin. "Of course I am, babe. I don't do anything by halves, Maggie. If I'm in, I'm all in."

She raises her eyebrows warily but there's a smile on her face. "I'm beginning to get that idea."

She dips the bacon in gooey egg yolk, and as she takes a large bite, her eyes close and her lips turn up in pleasure.

"Mmmm."

Here's a woman who appreciates her food. She's perfect, and I wonder how on earth I'm going to give her back after the weekend.

9
MAGGIE

My mouth is sore from laughing so much. I've spent the day with Arlo and my parents, and it's been happy and hilarious. We did the brewery tour, and after lunch we hiked one of the short trails that has an amazing view over the valley.

My parents were exhausted, so they went back to my place and I came back to Arlo's. He made spaghetti bolognaise for dinner, which we devoured while chatting easily. Now I'm making dessert while he watches me from his perch on a bar stool at the kitchen counter.

"When did you know you wanted to be a pastry chef?"

I stir the chocolate vigorously, checking for any lasting lumps. It's got to be just the right temperature when I pour it over the blueberry mousse which is on two plates before me.

"When I was about ten years old. I used to bake with Mom, and one of my cakes won a prize at our town fair. It was judged by one of those celebrity bakers from TV, and when they gave me the prize, she told me I had a talent and I should use it. I took her seriously. But it wasn't until culinary school that I realized desserts were really where it's at for me."

I take the pan off the stove top and focus on the pouring, letting the warm chocolate drizzle over the slice of mousse and then doing a zig zag pattern on the plate.

Arlo watches me intently, making my cheeks heat. I'm not used to being watched while I cook, but I don't mind his gaze on me.

There's chocolate left in the pan, and I put it back on the stove top and turn the heating element off. Then I spin one of the plates toward Arlo and hand him a fork.

"Voila."

He scoops some of the dessert onto the fork, and my gaze follows it to his lips. As soon as the flavors hit his taste buds his eyes close, and a satisfied groan comes out of his mouth.

My pussy flutters at the sounds he's making. I

never knew how sexy it could be watching a man enjoy a dessert you've made.

Captivated, I watch him take another forkful.

"This is good," he says between mouthfuls. "Really good."

I'm beaming as I bring a forkful to my mouth. The flavors explode on my tongue, and I let out a moan.

Arlo's watching me, and his eyes grow hooded. I know what that means, and my pussy clenches.

Memories of his face buried between my thighs slip into my mind. I look down quickly before he can read what I'm thinking about in my expression. I've never done anything so brazen before, but it felt right with Arlo.

He pushes his stool back and comes around the end of the counter and into the kitchen. He's so much bigger than me, and his body radiates a powerful male energy. His presence is so forceful that I back up against the kitchen counter.

"Is there any more?"

But it's not me he's come for, it's the dessert. I try not to let my disappointment show.

"Only the chocolate."

He reaches past me and takes the small pan from the stove top. I left the spoon in there, and when he takes it out chocolate dribbles off the end of it.

"You want some?"

He offers it to me, his eyes sparkling with mischief. I don't know what game he's playing, but if a hot man offers me melted chocolate, I'm not going to say no.

I move my head forward and open my mouth, but at the last minute Arlo jerks the spoon away. I glance up at him, and his eyes are sparkling with laughter.

I try again, and this time I'm too quick and capture the spoon in my mouth, but not before a trickle of chocolate lands on my chin.

"Let me."

Arlo leans forward and presses his mouth to the stray spot of chocolate. My breath hitches as he laps up the chocolate, nibbling on my lower lip and licking it off my skin.

Prickles of heat skitter across my body; my gaze meets his, and there's desire in his look. Desire and mischief.

He moves the spoon around the pan and holds up the chocolate laden spoon. It was hot when I was cooking, and all I'm wearing is my blouse with the top buttons undone. My breasts are pressed together, showing a valley of cleavage, and this is where he aims the spoon.

"What are you…?"

Before I can finish my sentence, warm gooey chocolate hits my skin. It trickles between the valley of my breasts, leaving a warm sticky trail.

"Whoops." Arlo chuckles. "I better get that."

His eyes are dancing, but I don't resist as he runs a finger over my chest and scoops up sticky chocolate. His touch has me on fire, and I want him so bad I whimper.

He chuckles at the sounds I make. And instead of licking the chocolate off his finger, he brings it to my mouth. His fingertip nudges my lips, looking for entry. My tongue flicks out and laps the chocolate off his finger while his gaze is on my lips, mesmerized as I suck his finger into my mouth, sucking off all the sweet chocolate until I swallow it down.

By the time his finger pops out of my mouth, we're both breathing hard.

I want Arlo. I can't deny it. We've agreed it's just for the weekend, because I can't give him any more than that. But I'll make damn sure I make the most of my weekend.

We move at the same time. Our mouths smash together as we rip at each other's clothes. He pulls my blouse off, sending buttons popping. They land on the floor and skitter across the kitchen. His mouth devours the chocolate on my skin as his fingers undo my bra.

Not bothering with the spoon, Arlo scoops chocolate onto his fingers and smears it over my breasts, leaving a sticky mess on my body.

Heat pools in my core, and my panties gush with my arousal. I've spent my life making desserts, and now I am the dessert.

What I love about cooking is not just the end result. I love the creation. I love the messiness of it. I pull Arlo toward me and rub my body against his, transferring chocolate sauce onto his torso. He's my favorite dessert and I lick him up, teasing his nipples with my tongue the way he does to me.

Then I'm pulling at his jeans, not sure what I want but knowing there's a need inside me that only he can fulfil.

He drags his jeans off and makes quick work of mine. We tumble to the kitchen floor in a mess of discarded clothes and chocolate.

"You're my favorite dessert." He swirls chocolate sauce around my nipples, and I stifle a cry as jolts of electricity course through my body.

His head moves down my stomach and I guess where he's heading, but I want more. I want to give him a good time. I want to eat him up for dessert too.

My hands tug at his boxers, and his huge cock pops out. I freeze. It's enormous. I've never seen a penis in the wild before, and this one's huge and erect and throbbing purple like a ripe blueberry. My core clenches as a pearl of pre-cum beads at the tip.

"It looks like a blueberry," I blurt out.

Arlo chuckles and sits back on his haunches.

"You could have said an eggplant. I'm not sure a blueberry is what a man wants his dick compared to."

I lick my lips, impatient for a taste. "Blueberry is my favorite fruit." I wiggle myself so that I'm positioned before him and pull him up to his knees. "It makes the best desserts."

The pan has been discarded on the floor, and I take a scoop of chocolate and dribble it on the tip of his cock.

Arlo gasps, and his eyes widen in surprise. I love that I can surprise him like this. I bet he's never had his dick made into dessert before.

Before he can say anything, I dip my head and lick the chocolate off his twitching cock. We groan at the same time.

I've never tasted anything so sweet. My tongue laps up the chocolate, making sure to lick every part of his shaft.

"Christ, Maggie, that feels good."

Encouraged by his words, I keep his cock in my

mouth as I reach for the chocolate, but he stops my hand.

"Let me take care of you."

I pop his cock out of my mouth but make sure to keep a firm hold on him. "Don't interrupt a girl when she's halfway through dessert," I warn him.

He chuckles. "You can finish dessert, Maggie, but I want a taste too."

He lies down on the floor and pulls me across him so that I'm straddling him backwards. "We can both enjoy dessert this way."

Heat floods my neck when I realize what he wants. Until yesterday I'd never done more than kiss a boy, and now I'm contemplating a sixty-niner on the kitchen floor.

His breath tickles my thighs and I wiggle into position, giving him access to my pussy while I reach for his cock.

The first lick has me squirming, and I can barely think straight. It feels so good I want to push down and writhe on his face until I come. But his blueberry cock glistens, and it's too tempting.

Getting a good lot of chocolate in my hands, I run it over his cock, coating it from shaft to tip. His moans reverberate against my clit, and I almost lose it.

Somehow I manage to concentrate long enough

to suck his cock into my mouth. I've never done this before and I'm sloppy, but he tastes so fucking good covered in chocolate and pre-cum.

I lick and I suck, and when my jaw gets sore, I lube my hands up with chocolate and run them down his shaft. From the noises Arlo makes, I can tell what he likes.

The pressure in my pussy builds until I can't stand it. Using my hands and my mouth I work his dick; my head bobs up and down, and my pussy grinds into his face. I'm so fucking close I can't stand it. But I want him to come too.

My movements get jerky as I lose focus. I'm sucking and tugging for all I'm worth. And then I explode. My pussy gushes all over his face, and at the same time his cock lengthens. Hot cum squirts out of the end of his cock. It hits the back of my throat, and cum and chocolate mixes in my mouth.

My tastebuds jerk at the sweet cream he pumps into my mouth. I swallow him down as my body convulses, lapping up every trace of chocolate and cum.

When I climb off Arlo, I'm sticky and happy and can't get the grin off my face. This is so much better than being at work.

The thought slams into my brain and makes me sit up hard on the wooden floor. I should have been at work today. Instead of making a mess on Arlo's floor, I could have been making a proper dessert.

This is how it starts. You miss a few days here and there, and then before you know it, someone else has come in and taken the promotion. Being a top chef is a competitive business, especially for a woman. If Travis thinks I've hooked up with Arlo, he'll think I'm not committed to the job.

The love bug has been going around the MC, and there are a bunch of pregnant women and happy men. Every single one of the guys who have found love recently have gotten their women pregnant in the first few months of being together. Travis will think that's what will happen with us, and he won't give the promotion to someone who's about to go off on maternity leave.

"You okay?"

Arlo's peering at me through lazy satisfied eyes.

"Yeah," I lie. I've just had the best experience of my life, but I can't repeat it. It's only for the weekend, I remind myself again.

"Come on." He stands up and helps me up. "Let's get in the shower and get cleaned up."

As I follow his perfectly rounded ass to the bathroom, a sadness settles on my chest. This is for the weekend. But that's all it can ever be. If I want a career, I can't have Arlo.

10

ARLO

Maggie's quiet when I bring her breakfast in bed the next morning. She gives me a tired smile like she didn't sleep much. I slept like a log with her in my arms.

I wish I could get behind her brown eyes and figure out what's going on in her head.

Last night was hands down the best night of my life. The sex was hot. But afterwards, once I'd washed her body in the shower and made her come again on the end of my tongue, I lay next to her in bed and held her as I fell asleep.

Holding her in my arms lifted my soul to a new level. I thought the sex was good, but nothing compares to sleeping next to the woman you love.

"When do your parents leave?"

She looks up from where she's pushing a piece of

bacon around the plate with her fork. She's not eaten much this morning.

"This afternoon."

I don't know if she's quiet because she's going to miss them, although I know how she feels about her mother. But I can't bear the thought of the weekend ending.

I sit next to her on the bed, and she raises those big brown eyes to mine.

"Maggie, this doesn't just have to be for the weekend. We could make this work."

She shakes her head, but not before I see a flash of longing in her eyes. She wants this as much as I do, but something's holding her back. She can't really believe she needs to choose between me and her career, can she?

"I can't allow that to happen. I told you that."

There's a sadness to her words, and I tilt her chin up so she has to look at me.

"Tell me you don't feel this, Maggie. This connection that's between us."

She shakes her head out of my grasp.

"No," she says defiantly. "I don't feel it."

The words make me sit back. She pulls the covers off and gets out of bed.

"I need to get back to work."

"You got the weekend off. I cleared it with Travis."

She turns at the door. "I don't want the weekend off. I don't want Travis to think I need time off, Arlo. I took this job to work. I want that promotion."

Determination blazes in her eyes. But it breaks my heart that she thinks she can't have both.

I follow her into the kitchen as she slams the breakfast tray onto the counter. The kitchen's still covered in chocolate mess from last night, and my dick twitches at the memory.

"It doesn't have to be like that, Maggie. Being with me doesn't mean giving up your job. You can have both. You deserve both."

She turns on me, and her eyes are wet with tears.

"You don't get it, Arlo. You're a man. Men can have both. But it's different for women. It wouldn't be fair to get involved with you."

She's exasperated like there's something I'm missing. We stare at each other.

"I don't want kids, Arlo. I don't want a family, so it's not fair to get involved with you."

The words have me reeling. I've been thinking about putting a baby in her belly since I first laid eyes on Maggie. But if it's not what she wants right away, I can wait.

"You don't have to think about kids now. Many women have them later in life."

She holds her hands out, stopping me in my tracks.

"No, Arlo, you don't get it. I don't want kids ever. My career will always come first. And I won't let you give that up for me. I should never have asked you to pretend for my parents. I'm sorry."

My fantasies of Maggie in my cabin, overrun by laughing children, shatter.

I take a step towards her; I can't believe she can just walk away after what we've shared in the last few days.

"Please…"

She puts her hand up again. "Just drop me back at the restaurant. I left my car there on Friday. I'm going to work, I'm going to see my parents, and that's it. We'll go back to how we were before. Colleagues and nothing more."

My heart shatters into a hundred pieces. She turns away and heads to the bedroom. But I'm too stunned to follow. I've never met anyone so determined and so infuriatingly stubborn.

Maggie comes out a few moments later fully dressed, and I silently pick up my keys.

"I'm sorry it didn't work out like you wanted, Arlo."

"Life doesn't always work out, Maggie. That's the point. If you get a shot at happiness, you should take it. Because you don't know what's going to work out and what's not."

I don't wait for a reply. I grab the helmets and head out to the bike.

She wants me to drop her off. That's what I'll do, but I'll be damned if I'm giving up on her.

11
MAGGIE

"Try to get to the hairdresser once in a while, will you, MeMe?"

Mom pats the top of my head forlornly as if it's got a personality of its own and it's a wayward teenager.

"I'll try." I duck my head out of her reach and scoot around her to where Dad's wrangling the suitcases. I give him a big hug, and we share a look.

"Take care of yourself." His eyes are full of concern, picking up on the heaviness that's settled on me.

"I'm going to take these to the car." Dad wheels the suitcases out the door, and I'm left with Mom.

There's a churning in my gut that I've felt all day. I did the lunch shift at work; Travis was surprised to see me, but no one turned down the extra help in the kitchen.

I met my parents in the afternoon and had to listen to Mom go on about how great Allan is and when we'll be having babies.

This charade was supposed to get her off my back, but all I've done is make her more impatient for grandkids.

"Look after Allan, won't you?"

She's peering at me like she knows something's wrong, and suddenly I can't take it anymore. I've made a mess out of everything, and I'm done pretending.

"His name's Arlo."

Mom tilts her head and eyes me suspiciously. "I thought it was Allan."

I shake my head. "No Mom. And he's not my boyfriend either."

Her mouth drops open.

"Maggie, what happened? I thought you were off today. Did you two break up? It's not because we're here, is it?"

I close my eyes and wait for her to stop talking while a headache forms behind my forehead. When she finally does, I speak.

"He was never my boyfriend, Mom."

She's quiet for a long moment, and for the first

time in my life I wish she'd say something. Finally she sucks in her breath.

"Well, I thought you were acting strange."

I hate the hurt on her face, but now that I've started telling the truth, it all comes out.

"I pretended he was my boyfriend because I wanted you to stop hassling me about having kids."

Mom's mouth drops open. "I do not hassle you."

Typical of Mom to be so oblivious.

"You do, Mom. Every time I talk to you, you ask me when you're gonna get grandkids. You keep talking about Layla having babies. I thought if I pretended I had a boyfriend, you'd stop harassing me."

Her mouth opens and closes like a fish. "So, you're telling me you don't have a boyfriend?"

"No, Mom. And I don't want one. My job's too important to me."

"Oh, honey, I know it's important to you. I'm so proud of you. I never got to have a career. And here's you, working at this fancy restaurant."

It's my turn to be surprised. I've never once heard Mom say she was proud of what I do.

"So you mean to tell me that Allan... Arlo was pretending all this time?"

I think about his lips crushing mine, the way his

eyes light up when he smiles, and the taste of his dick in my mouth.

"Yes Mom, he was pretending. Sorry."

She raises her eyebrows at me. "Well, if he's been pretending, he should go to Hollywood, MeMe. There is nothing fake about the way that man looks at you."

My breath catches at her words, and there's a longing deep inside me.

"I know you want your career, MeMe. But a love like that only comes around once in a lifetime. You gotta grab it with both hands. If he loves you, you'll figure out the work life balance."

My mouth drops open. It's the first time Mom has ever mentioned anything about a work life balance. All she's ever talked about was how my career will ruin my family life.

"I'm proud of you, MeMe, and what you've done with your career. But please, don't let that man get away. And I'm not saying that because I want grandbabies. I'm saying that because I want you to be happy.

"The way that man looks at you reminds me of me and your father when we were younger." A faraway look comes into her eyes. "You know what we used to do… "

"No Mom." I stop her before she can say something inappropriate. "I don't want to know what you and Dad used to get up to."

She chuckles, a throaty laugh. "Just as well, honey. You blush too easily anyway."

"Are you ready, love?" Dad calls from the doorway.

Mom pats my cheek and smiles.

"Whatever you do with your life, MeMe, we're real proud of you. And I promise not to mention grandbabies again."

I raise an eyebrow at her. "Really?"

Mom considers. "Well, I promise only to mention them once a week."

It's a start.

Mum clatters down the steps and gets into the car. Dad honks the horn as they pull away and turn onto the mountain road.

I go back into my apartment and shut the door, letting out a long sigh. The only sound is the ticking of the clock and the muffled sound of a television from the apartment next door.

In my too small kitchen, I find a leftover piece of chocolate cake in the fridge. I grab a fork and sit on the couch, spooning forkfuls of it into my mouth.

All my life I wanted something different than what Mom had. I've wanted to get away from her overbearing personality and smothering love. But all

I've done is push away the one person I've ever felt anything for.

There's a knock at the door, and I put the cake down. I cast my eyes around the room to see what it is Mom's forgotten. But I can't see anything. When I pull open the door, it's not Mom, but Arlo, looking ruggedly handsome in his biker jacket and rough beard.

My heart skips a beat at the sight of him.

"Can I come in?"

I step back, letting him in, and he strides into my apartment, taking up all the space and reminding me how small it is.

"Do you want some cake?"

I grab him a fork from the kitchen, and we sit on the couch. He seems nervous, his foot tapping.

There're so many things I want to say to him. I open my mouth to tell him that I might have made a mistake, but he gets there first.

"Maggie. I know you think you can't have love and a career. But that is not true."

He takes my hands in his, and then he sinks to one knee in front of me on the couch. The breath goes out of me when I realize what he's doing.

"If you marry me, I will support you one hundred percent. I will not get in the way of your career, and I will help you in any way I can to achieve what you want to achieve. You're an amazing chef, and I want you to have everything you deserve, and I want to be the support that will get you there."

I go to speak, and he holds up his hand.

"I know you don't want children, and that's okay, if that's what you decide. You're enough for me, babydoll. But let me tell you something. All those male chefs that you compare yourself to, they have families. Who do you think looks after the kids? There'll be two parents in this relationship, Maggie. And if I need to step up and be a full time dad so that you can achieve your dreams, then that's what I'll do. So, what do you say?"

He takes a ring out of his pocket It's a blue amethyst surrounded by sparkling diamonds, a perfect little blueberry.

"Will you marry me?"

Tears sting my eyes, and my heart opens. He's offering me everything I ever wanted, but I realize the thing I want most of all is him.

I see a future that I didn't dare to dream of. But that's not why I say yes. I say yes because the alternate future without him is too painful to think about.

"I don't want to live without you, Arlo. Even if I have to give up cooking, I want to be with you."

He smiles and cups my cheek in his hand.

"Babe, I don't ever wanna hear you say that again. You aren't giving up shit for me, alright? I'm gonna support you one hundred percent to be the best damned pastry chef in the state. So, what do you say?"

My eyes get lost in his, and my heart is full. "Yes!" I throw my arms around his neck. "Yes, yes, yes!"

Arlo slides the ring on my finger as he climbs over me onto the couch. He pulls me down, and I squeal.

"You just made me the happiest man alive."

He pulls me close, and I grind myself against him.

"There's only one thing that would make me happier," I say.

He pulls back and looks me in the eye. "You name it, sweetheart, and it's all yours."

I bite my lower lip. "I had a taste of blueberry. Now, do you want some cherry pie?"

12
ARLO

I pull Maggie to her feet, and my hands hook around her waist. Her feet stumble over each other as I drag her to the bed in the corner of the room. My pint sized fiancé giggles as I throw her onto the bed.

"I'm going to destroy that cherry pie."

She scurries back onto the bed, but before she gets too far, I grab her ankle and pull her toward me. She squeals with delight and immediately clamps her hand over her mouth, reminding of another thing I'm determined to do.

"By the time I'm done with you, you'll be screaming my name. No more hiding your light, beautiful."

She looks scandalized. "I've got neighbors, and these walls are thin," she whispers.

"I don't care. You'll be moving into my cabin right after I'm done with you." I climb onto the bed and push her legs apart with my thighs.

"You want to be a master chef, you need confidence, and I'm gonna coax that out of you."

She bites her lower lip as my hand slides up her skirt. Her thighs are creamy and soft and she parts them for me, letting my hand slide right up until I hook my fingers over the band of her panties.

Her panties come off with a jerk of my hand, and I bury myself between her legs. She gasps at the suddenness of it and grasps the duvet in her fist.

It's only been two days, but this is already my favorite dish. I can't get enough of my girl, and I lick her and suck her until she's panting hard.

Maggie's whimpers as she grinds her pussy into my face, shooting her cream onto my tongue as she comes.

I let her off the first time, but the next time she comes she'll be screaming my name.

There's a condom in my pocket. I'm prepared to respect her wishes. No matter how much I want a baby in her belly, I'll respect what Maggie wants.

She shakes her head when she sees the condom.

"I'm on the pill."

Her words make me smile. I don't want anything between us.

I climb up the bed, shredding my clothes as she tugs at hers. Our lips collide, and there's a frantic energy about the way her hands clasp my cock.

I sit back and pause, panting hard but wanting to savor this moment. She's splayed out before me, her juices glistening on her thighs, her eyes wide and dark with desire. The only thing she's wearing is the ring on her finger, and a wave of emotion rushes over me.

"I love you, Maggie." Her eyes meet mine.

"I love you too," she whispers.

With our eyes locked I slowly slide into her, sucking my breath in as her pussy sucks my cock into its tight walls.

My tip grazes her virgin barrier, and I pause. A nervous look passes across her face; she's vulnerable right now and trusting.

"This may hurt, babydoll."

My hand closes over hers on the bed, and our fingers lock. Slowly, I slide into her soft cherry pie. She clenches around me, and her jaw locks as she hisses between her teeth. Typical Maggie to let the pain out quietly.

"I want you to make some noise for me, Maggie. If it hurts, you scream. If it feels good, you scream. You got it?"

She nods, still looking tense.

"I need to hear your words, babydoll." As I say it, I rock my hips and she moans.

"You understand?"

"Yes." It's a breathless yes and barely above a whisper.

"Louder, sweetheart."

As I say it, I rock my hips and she moans.

"Yes." It's a little louder but not good enough.

"Louder."

This time I thrust deep into her and grab a nipple in my mouth. She gasps, then remembers her words.

"Yes!"

Her voice echoes around the walls of the apartment, and I hope the fucker next door watching annoying television shows all day hears her.

I clutch her hips and I sway slowly until I feel her pussy relax around me. My fingers flick her nipples, and I lean forward to kiss her swollen lips.

I rock gently, loving the way she wraps herself against my body as she gets into the rhythm.

Her pussy feels like heaven, but I want to go deeper. I want to her to feel all of me.

I grab her legs and throw them over my shoulder, and she gasps as I drive my cock home. Her face scrunches up.

"Make some noise, Maggie," I command.

Her eyes fly open, and her mouth forms a perfect O.

I thrust deep and she lets out a startled cry, the sound piercing the silence of the apartment.

"That's it, honey. Make some noise for me."

Her tits jiggle as I slam into her, bouncing her around on the bed. I'm fucking her hard, but I can't stop myself.

"I want everyone to know who's fucking you. You say my name, and you say it loud."

Her brow furrows and I pull back, making her whimper.

My thumb circles her clit, and she gives another cry.

"Arlo…"

My name on my lips almost makes me lose it, and I pull myself almost the whole way out of her before I come too soon.

She lifts her head off the pillow, the perspiration making her hair cling to her forehead.

"I like… please…"

"Please what?"

I'm enjoying the frustration in her look. The disbelief that I've taken her toy away from her.

"I want to come," she whispers.

"You can come, Maggie. As soon as you scream my name."

Her eyes dart around the empty apartment.

"But my neighbors."

"They're not gonna be your neighbors for very long. As soon as we're done here, I'm packing your bags and taking you to my cabin."

Her eyes go wide.

"Are you gonna be this demanding and bossy when we're married?"

"You know it. You can run your career how you want. I'm gonna run the household."

She's about to sass me back when I give her a hard thrust. My balls slam against her asshole, and I almost lose it. Whatever she's gonna say dies on her lips.

"Oh," she pants.

"That's it, baby."

My thumb presses against her clit and I thrust hard, enjoying the way her pussy sucks onto my cock.

"I'm close," she whimpers.

"Good girl. Come for me, Maggie. Come for me loud and hard."

I pull back a little, and she gives me desperate look. But I want to make her come so hard. I want to push her to the edge.

She starts to whimper and I slam into her, leaning forward so our bodies are pressed together.

"Say my name, Maggie."

"Arlo..." she whimpers.

"Louder."

"Arlo," she cries.

My name on her lips in her strained voice is my undoing.

"Fuck Maggie....

I slam into her as her pussy convulses around me.

"Arlo," she screams. "Arlo, Arlo, Arlo!"

My balls tighten and I shoot cum straight into her, growling out her name so our voices bounce off the walls of the apartment. My body trembles with hers as I give her everything I've got.

My arms close around her, and I pull her close as we fall exhausted onto the bed.

The silence in the apartment is deafening. The television next door is off for the first time, and I hope they enjoyed the fucking sound show.

Maggie turns her wide eyes to me and giggles.

"Do you think the neighbors heard?"

"I don't give a shit. Like I said, you're moving in with me."

She giggles again. "It's Larry who lives next door. You know, the guy who runs the convenience store. I'm going to be embarrassed every time I go in to buy milk."

I throw my head back and laugh.

"Well then, let's give you something to really be embarrassed about."

I roll her on top of me, and my dick hardens when she wiggles against me.

"So where is this secret tattoo?" She runs her fingertips up my thighs and over my balls.

"You'll have to find it," I tease. "But you're close."

As my future wife slides down my cock, I'm filled with a sense of happiness. Her moans echo around the room, and they're a sound I'm going to enjoy hearing for the rest of my life.

EPILOGUE

MAGGIE

Four years later…

"Hurry up," I whine while pulling Arlo through the back door of the industrial kitchen and into the stock cupboard. I tug at the corner of his dinner jacket with one hand and clasp my gold trophy in the other.

The door slams closed behind us, throwing us into near darkness. Arlo pushes me against the shelving unit as his mouth closes over mine.

My arms slide around his neck, kissing him with a hunger that's made more intense by the dizzy high I'm on.

"We shouldn't be in here," I say feebly, even though I'm the one that led him here.

My pussy flutters as he spins me away from the

shelves and backs me up against the wall. He nudges my legs apart with his thighs and hikes up the satin dress I'm wearing. His other hand runs down the strapless back and over the shiny fabric to clasp my buttocks.

"Aren't I allowed to congratulate my wife?"

His hands brush against my panties, which are already soaked, making me whimper.

"I'm so proud of you, babydoll," he says, stroking my wet panties.

"You should be. I just won an award based on a dessert named after you."

My blueberry explosion just won me the North Carolina Pastry Chef award.

I've been working toward this for the last four years, and I couldn't be happier. As Head Pastry Chef at the Wild Taste Restaurant and Bar, I've been allowed free rein to experiment.

My desserts have become famous in the area. One more reason for tourists to visit our side of the mountain.

The award is the cherry on top, and I'm on a natural high, which is why I've dragged my husband into a random storage closet at the awards venue.

Even Mom came to watch the ceremony, her eyes glistening with tears when my name was called out. She'll be wondering where we've gotten to, but she'll just have to wait. It's not Mom I'm thinking of as Arlo pulls aside the gusset of my panties.

"Watching you up on stage getting that award turned me on so much." He unzips his dress pants, and I slide his hard cock into my hand. "Nothing makes me harder than seeing my wife succeed."

I give a sigh of contentment as I brush the tip of his cock over my opening. He's the most supportive husband a girl could wish for, and I honestly don't think I could have gotten where I am today without his love and support. I thought I needed to do this alone, but without Arlo, I wouldn't be here.

Which is why I'm going to give him the one thing he really wants.

My sigh turns to a gasp as he thrusts roughly into me. He pulls my hips towards him, sliding my pussy down his cock. I bite my lower lip to stop from crying out. The last thing I want to do is get found making out in the supply closet at the awards ceremony.

But any thoughts flee my mind as his hips piston, slamming his cock in and out of my pussy. My dress is pushed up around my waist, and with every thrust my back hits the wall. It's quick and dirty, and the pressure builds inside me like the champagne in the bottle we just consumed.

Arlo pants my name as he picks up the pace. It's

been four years since we got married, but we're still as passionate for each other as the day that we got together.

Arlo really brought me out of my shell. I'm not the shy girl I was before we met, too afraid to stand up to her own mother. With Arlo by my side, I feel invincible, like I can do anything.

I'm still clasping the award with one hand as he slams into me, and with my other hand I grab hold of his shoulder.

Pleasure bubbles to the surface, but I want to give him his present before we both come.

"There's something I need to tell you." I pant the words between thrusts.

"Better make it quick, honey, because I'm about to render you speechless."

He tilts my hips so his dick sinks deeper into me, and for a moment I can't speak. I'm so close to coming, but I need to get this out.

"I've stopped taking the pill."

He freezes mid thrust just as the bubbles of pleasure explode out of me. I cling onto him, rocking onto his dick as my nails dig into his shoulder.

When I open my eyes, Arlo's staring at me.

"You're serious?"

My chest constricts, wondering if I've made a mistake. Arlo's always wanted children, but we haven't talked about it for a while. He's never pressured me. But lately, I've been wondering what it would be like to have a little Arlo running around. How a little family would make life complete.

But maybe it's not what he wants anymore.

"Is it still what you want?"

A grin spreads across his face. He pulls his hips back and slams into me so hard my teeth rattle.

"I'm going to be a daddy."

"Not yet," I pant as he starts fucking me with a new vigor.

"I'm gonna plant my seed in you today, babydoll. Your belly is going to be round and fat by the end of the summer."

He's fucking me hard now, and I love that he's so turned on by this. Without warning, my pussy explodes again. And as I come, so does he, with a feral grunt as his sperm shoots deep into my belly.

He holds me for a long time, making sure I get every last drop before carefully sliding himself out and putting my panties back in place.

He tugs me to the floor of the closet.

"What are you doing?"

"Sit down with your legs in the air. We're not wasting a drop, Maggie."

I giggle but do as I'm told. My gold heels stick up

in the air, but there's a stern look on his face which stops me from arguing.

"So, you still want to be a father?"

"Babe, I've been looking forward to this ever since I met you. I can't wait to get you pregnant. We're going to have the most beautiful babies. And if they're anything like their mother, they'll be smart and talented too. Now sit."

He crouches beside me in the store cupboard, his shoulders knocking against some stacked boxes.

My hand clasps his, and I rest my head on his shoulder. We sit like that for a long time, Arlo talking quietly about the adjustments to the cabin he's going to make to get it ready for children.

I can't believe I thought I had to choose between a career or love. With Arlo in one hand and my trophy in the other, I'm grateful that I got both.

* * *

BONUS SCENE

Want more of Maggie and Arlo? Find out what happens when Maggie finally accepts she can have a family and a career.

Get the Wild Curves bonus scene for a snap shot of family life with Maggie and Arlo.

Read the bonus scene when you sign up to the Sadie King mailing list.

To sign up visit:

authorsadieking.com/bonus-scenes

Already a subscriber? Check your last email for the link to access all the bonus content.

WHAT TO READ NEXT

His military training didn't prepare him for life as a single dad...

There was a surprise waiting for me when I got back from the military. A screaming, pooping, noisy surprise.

I'm a hard man, a biker who loves the quiet of the mountains. But my quiet life is shattered by the infant who's relying on me.

Her mother passed, and I'm all she has . . . until her aunt turns up trying to get custody of my baby.

April would be infuriating if she wasn't so hot.

But where was she when the baby needed her family? And why has she only just surfaced now?

Wild Forever is a single dad, found family, age gap romance featuring an ex-military biker mountain man and the curvy, innocent woman he makes his forever.

WILD FOREVER

EXCERPT

April

The stranger, Grant, smiles too much. It peeps through his beard and lights up his pale blue eyes, and every time he does it, I feel a twinge in my core.

Which is the last thing I need right now.

I'm on a mission, and there's no time to get distracted by a hot man in leather straddling a bike.

Not even one that has a tattoo peeping out from the top of his t-shirt that clings to his muscular chest under his jacket.

He's got red flags all over him, the kind of guy my caseworker would tell me to steer clear of. But like a fool, I'm contemplating his offer for a lift.

But what choice do I have?

I messed up the train timings and got to Hope late. Then I stupidly went for a walk along the river instead of waiting for the bus. But my back ached and needed a stretch, and now it still aches and needs a rest.

My fingers itch, and I scape them against my jeans.

Visualize your happy place.

I hear my therapist's voice in my head. It's her solution for when anything gets complicated.

With this bearded biker looking at me with intense curiosity and heat in his gaze, I think I just found my new happy place.

"Are you visiting someone in Wild?" he asks.

It's a fair question, but I'm not sure how to answer it. "I'm on vacation."

Which isn't exactly a lie.

He stares at me, this time managing to keep his gaze from my chest. Although I have to admit, I don't mind him checking me out.

My cheeks heat as he watches me. I'm not used to being looked at like this, like I'm somebody worth looking at.

"Most people stay in Hope. It's got the river and the shops. Why Wild? It's a bit off the beaten track."

Damn, he's asking too many questions. I stand up

off the boulder, clenching my teeth when my back bites. It's been good lately, but six hours on a train has triggered the old pain.

"I like being off the beaten track."

I reach for my bag, hoping he gets the hint and doesn't ask any more questions, but before I get my backpack, he gets there first. Our fingers brush, and a spark of electricity jumps between us. It makes me gasp and I pull my hand back quickly, my eyes darting to his. He looks as shocked as I do, so he must have felt it too.

I turn away quickly. The last thing I need is to finally find a man I'm attracted to. Not here, not now.

He stuffs my bag into his saddle bag and takes the shopping bag as well. He looks at the Babyland bag and I can tell he's about to ask questions, so I cut him off.

"Do you know the Wild Times Hotel in Wild?"

"It's the only hotel in town." He frowns. "It's above the bar. Not a nice place for a girl like you."

I fold my arms and study him. He has no idea what kind of girl I am, but I appreciate the concern. Maybe a little too much.

"Get on, and I'll take you there."

He pulls the helmet off his head and slides it onto

mine. His fingers adjust the catch, and when his fingertips brush my skin, heat skitters across my body and my pulse ramps up a notch.

His eyes meet mine, and there's a mischievous glint to them as if he knows exactly what effect he's having on me.

"I didn't catch your name?"

There's no way I'm giving out my name, not until I get what I came for. I match his grin, going for a flirty tone.

"I don't give out my name to strangers."

It doesn't quite come out as lighthearted as I intended, but he chuckles anyway, and I'm relieved when he doesn't press me.

"You been on a bike before?"

I nod, and he frowns. Is that jealousy I see flash across his features? In a moment it's gone, and the jovial smile is back. I must have imagined it.

"Hold onto me and enjoy the view."

We peel out of the overlook lot and onto the road that heads out of town and into the mountains. I cling to his waist, breathing in the heady scent of leather and mountain pine.

I must be crazy. I know I'm crazy. This entire scheme of mine is crazy, the act of a desperate woman. I don't think I was thinking straight when I left home this morning.

But as I cling onto Grant, my head feels clear. Whatever happens this weekend, at least I got a ride on a motorbike behind a hot biker.

To keep reading visit:
mybook.to/WHMCWildForever

BOOKS AND SERIES BY SADIE KING

Wild Heart Mountain

Military Heroes

Wild Riders MC

Mountain Heroes

Temptation

A Runaway Bride for Christmas

A Secret Baby for Christmas

Sunset Coast

Underground Crows MC

Sunset Security

Men of the Sea

Love and Obsession - The Cod Cove Trilogy

His Christmas Obsession

Maple Springs

Small Town Sisters

Candy's Café

All the Single Dads

Men of Maple Mountain

All the Scars we Cannot See

What the Fudge

Fudge and the Firefighter

The Seal's Obsession

His Big Book Stack

For a full list of Sadie King's books check out her website

www.authorsadieking.com

ABOUT THE AUTHOR

Sadie King is a USA Today Best Selling Author of contemporary romance novellas.

She lives in New Zealand with her ex-military husband and raucous young son.

When she's not writing she loves catching waves with her son, running along the beach, and drinking good wine with a book in hand.

Keep in touch when you sign up for her newsletter. You'll snag yourself a free short romance and access to all the bonus content!

authorsadieking.com/bonus-scenes